ZOMBIE INVASION

ZOMBIE INVASION

MINECRAFTERS ACADEMY

BOOK ONE

Winter Morgan

Sky Pony Press
New York

Copyright © 2016 by Hollan Publishing, Inc.

Minecraft® is a registered trademark of Notch Development AB.

The Minecraft game is copyright © Mojang AB.

This book is not authorized or sponsored by Microsoft Corp., Mojang AB, Notch Development AB or Scholastic Inc., or any other person or entity owning or controlling rights in the Minecraft name, trademark, or copyrights.

Sky Pony Press books may be purchased in bulk at special discounts for sales promotion, corporate gifts, fund-raising, or educational purposes. Special editions can also be created to specifications. For details, contact the Special Sales Department, Sky Pony Press, 307 West 36th Street, 11th Floor, New York, NY 10018 or info@skyhorsepublishing.com.

Sky Pony® is a registered trademark of Skyhorse Publishing, Inc.®, a Delaware corporation.

Minecraft® is a registered trademark of Notch Development AB.
The Minecraft game is copyright © Mojang AB.

Visit our website at www.skyponypress.com.

10 9 8 7 6 5 4 3 2 1

Library of Congress Cataloging-in-Publication Data is available on file.

Cover photo by Megan Miller
Cover design by Brian Peterson

Print ISBN: 978-1-5107-0594-4
Ebook ISBN: 978-1-5107-0604-0

Printed in Canada

TABLE OF CONTENTS

ZOMBIE INVASION

Chapter 1
THE INVITATION

Lucy couldn't believe she had been accepted to Minecrafters Academy. She had always dreamt about attending the prestigious school. At Minecrafters Academy, you learned how to build majestic homes, brew special potions, and hunt for resources that were vital for survival in the Overworld. She would be one among the elite students at the academy, and Lucy was thrilled. Although, she had to admit, she was also a little nervous. She wouldn't have her friends, Max, Henry, and Steve with her. She would have to make new friends.

Lucy sprinted over to her friends, Max and Henry, who were helping Steve work on his wheat farm. They were working with him to create a new irrigation system so his crops would grow faster.

Lucy called out, "I just got a letter from Minecrafters Academy!"

"What does it say?" asked Steve.

"They want me to study there."

"When do you leave?" asked Henry.

"Tomorrow." Lucy could barely believe the words coming from her own mouth. She had so little time to prepare. She was beginning to grow quite anxious. There was so much to do. Her inventory needed to be stocked, and she had to make sure she had an enchantment table and the many other tools required for all students at the academy.

"Tomorrow? That's so soon." Henry looked shocked.

"I know. I feel a bit overwhelmed. There is so much to do to prepare for the trip." Lucy began to pace.

"That means you won't be able to go on the treasure hunt I had planned." Max was disappointed. They had discussed going on a treasure hunt to the Nether. Someone had told Max about an amazing treasure in a Nether fortress. They had been planning to leave the next day to search for the fortress and unearth the treasure.

"I know." Lucy was very disappointed, too. "But when I get back, I'll be able to help find all sorts of treasures. Just think of the new skills I'll learn when I'm away."

"I know," said Max. "But we are going to miss you. You're a part of our team."

Henry added, "The treasure hunts aren't going to be the same without you."

Lucy was upset. She didn't want to make her friends sad, but she knew this was an opportunity that she couldn't pass up. "I am going to miss you guys a lot. But I bet the time will fly by."

Steve said, "Isn't Minecrafters Academy far from here?'

"Yes, that's why I have to leave tomorrow. I want to give myself enough time to make the journey," Lucy replied.

Steve suggested, "Can we accompany you on the trip to the academy?"

"Yes." Lucy was so happy. She had been worried about traveling there alone. To get there, you had to travel through various biomes, and it would take a few days. Now she would have help crafting homes and battling any hostile mobs or griefers she might encounter on her trip.

"I'd also like to help you stock up your inventory. As you know, I have a lot of resources, and I want to share them with you," Steve told Lucy. Steve was a successful wheat farmer and he traded his wheat for various resources.

"Thanks, Steve!" Lucy was so happy to have such good friends. She knew that despite being far away for a long stretch of time, they would still be friends.

"It's getting dark," Henry remarked. "We should head back to the farmhouse. We don't want to battle any hostile mobs."

"Too late," Max announced as he watched two lanky Endermen walk past them.

Lucy reassured Max, "There's nothing to worry about. If we don't stare at the Endermen, they won't attack us."

Although this was true, Henry had accidently looked in the direction of one of the two dark block-carrying Endermen, and the purple-eyed beast let out a shriek and teleported toward him.

Henry stood frozen in terror. He didn't want to battle the Enderman. It had been a long day, and he had spent a large portion of the day helping Steve tend to his wheat farm.

"Help!" Henry called out to the others.

"Sprint toward the water!" Lucy instructed Henry.

Henry sprinted as fast as he could in the direction of the water. His friends followed him.

"Jump in!" Max shouted to Henry.

Henry jumped into the deep, blue water and both of the Endermen followed closely behind.

"Henry, are you okay?" Lucy called out.

Henry swam to the shore. "The Endermen were destroyed. It's going to be okay, but we have to head back to Steve's house. We need to get inside. It's getting darker and I fear that we will be attacked again."

"Oh no!" Lucy called out. "Zombies!"

Zombies lumbered toward them. A group of townspeople sprinted behind them, attacking them with swords and arrows. One of the townspeople called out, "We need help! The village is being attacked by hordes of zombies."

Henry looked over at Lucy. "I guess this is going to be a memorable last night."

"You're right." Lucy smiled as she and her friends sprinted toward the village armed with diamond swords and bows and arrows.

Kaboom!

An explosion was heard in the distance.

Henry cried out, "I think we're going to be fighting a lot more than zombies."

Max clutched his diamond sword. "It sounds like the village is under attack."

Kaboom!

A second explosion was heard throughout the town.

Lucy shouted to a townsperson, "Do you know who is behind this attack?"

"No, but I think someone is blowing up all the stores in the town with TNT."

"It sounds like a griefer," said Max.

"We can't just make a guess. We have to take action," Henry called out to his friends as he sprinted toward the town. He was ready to battle the zombies and find out who was behind the explosions.

Chapter 2
HERE COMES TROUBLE

As Lucy sprinted with her friends, she secretly worried that the battle would take too long and she wouldn't be able to make it to the academy on time. But she had to stop thinking about herself, because there was a village to save. When she entered the town, Lucy noticed her friend Eliot the Blacksmith's shop had been destroyed by TNT. She looked for Eliot. She feared for his safety. Her heart began to beat quickly.

"Eliot!" Lucy called out, but there was no response.

Henry looked over at Lucy. "We have to see if he's okay."

They tried to battle zombies as they searched for their missing friend.

"Watch out!" Henry cried as a zombie lurked behind Lucy.

Lucy turned and attacked the zombie with her diamond sword. Two more zombies approached her and she struck them as well. With a few blows from her sword, she was able to destroy the zombies.

"Oh no!" Steve sounded terrified. "I can't believe how many zombies are spawning."

"Somebody must be behind this attack," Lucy called out as she struck three more zombies and destroyed them.

Henry reminded them, "We have to find Eliot."

Lucy agreed, but the village was filled with zombies. The vacant-eyed beasts ripped the doors from their hinges and attacked the helpless villagers inside the shops and library. As the villagers were being transformed into zombie villagers, Lucy looked through her inventory for golden apples to help save them. While searching through her inventory, she heard a familiar voice.

"Lucy!" It was Eliot!

"Eliot! Are you okay?"

"Yes, but after my shop was destroyed, I saw someone dressed in a blue suit carrying blocks of TNT. I tried to follow them, but I lost them. They were headed toward Steve's wheat farm. You have to stop them. They could blow up his house," Eliot informed his friends.

Two zombies lumbered toward Eliot. Lucy took out her bow and arrow and aimed at the zombies. "We have to find the griefers and stop them from destroying Steve's house." Lucy was upset.

Steve was in the middle of battling five zombies. He was outnumbered and couldn't concentrate. He was worried about his home. He had worked so hard to build his farmhouse, and he'd be devastated if zombies destroyed it.

Kaboom!

"Oh no!" Lucy called out. "I hope that wasn't your home, Steve."

Steve couldn't respond. He was battling the zombies with his diamond sword and fighting for his survival. Lucy destroyed a zombie that lunged at her and quickly joined Steve in his battle against the zombies that surrounded him.

"Why are all of these zombies spawning?" Lucy asked breathlessly as she fought alongside Steve.

"I'm going to search for the spawner," Henry alerted his friends.

"Do you need help?" asked Lucy.

"Yes, come with me," Henry replied.

Lucy and Henry sprinted up the mountain and searched for the zombie spawner, but they couldn't find it.

"Ouch!" Lucy cried as an arrow struck her arm.

"Skeletons!" Henry pointed at four skeletons that were in the distance.

"We'll never find the spawner now." Lucy felt defeated. They had to battle these skeletons, and they were losing energy quickly.

Lucy leapt at the skeletons with her sword. She used all her might to destroy two skeletons as Henry obliterated the other two bony beasts.

"We have to help our friends," said Lucy. "Let's get out of here."

"We have to find the spawner or this zombie invasion will never end." Henry sprinted away from the town and in the direction of the zombies.

"I don't think we're going to find it." Lucy could hear the cries from the village. She felt helpless as they traveled further from their town, eventually reaching the jungle biome.

"I see a jungle temple! I bet the spawner is in the dungeon." Henry sprinted toward the fortress.

Three zombies approached them, and a zombie struck Lucy. She was losing energy quickly. "Help!"

Henry leapt at the zombies and destroyed them with his sword. He quickly gave Lucy some milk to restore her energy.

"This is a tough battle," Lucy said and took a sip of milk. "I wanted to spend the night preparing for academy. I didn't expect to battle zombies."

"We're almost at the jungle temple." Henry reassured Lucy that it would be okay and the battle was almost over.

"You're right. And I couldn't leave the village in this state. I'd feel too guilty," Lucy added.

As the duo approached the jungle temple, they saw an army of zombies walk out. Quickly, they hid behind a large tree.

"I think we found it," Henry whispered.

"We have to go inside." Lucy sprinted into the temple, narrowly avoiding being attacked by the zombies. Together they raced down the stairs and toward the dungeon.

"I found the spawner!" Henry called out.

Lucy grabbed torches from her inventory and set them up around the spawner while Henry built bedrock walls to contain it.

"It's done!" Lucy was excited. The zombie invasion would be over. They sprinted back to town to inform their friends of the fantastic news, but their friends were too busy battling the remaining zombies to pay attention to Lucy and Henry.

Lucy and Henry joined their friends in battle. They used their diamond swords to annihilate a large group of zombies. With each zombie they destroyed, they knew the battle was almost over.

"We destroyed the final zombie," Steve called out. Everyone was exhausted, but happy the battle was won.

"We destroyed the spawner," Henry told them.

"Maybe this battle is finally over." Max sounded hopeful.

The sun was rising. Lucy wanted to head back to Steve's farmhouse and prepare for the trip. "We have to go back to the house," she said.

Steve said nervously, "I hope my farmhouse wasn't blown up."

They sprinted back to the house. They didn't know what they would find.

Chapter 3
THE TRIP

As the gang sprinted toward Steve's house, they saw a large hole in the ground.

"Your wheat was destroyed." Max looked down at the crater.

"That's awful. After all the work we did. You spent all day helping me build the irrigation system." Steve inspected the area.

"I wonder who is behind all of this trouble." Max stood next to Steve and looked at the damaged crops.

"We will get to the bottom of this," said Henry, "but first we have to help Lucy get to Minecrafters Academy. If she doesn't leave today, she will be late for the first day of school."

Lucy thanked them. "I am so happy we will be traveling together."

"Let's go back to my house and help you prepare," suggested Steve.

The gang walked into the farmhouse. Steve was relieved the TNT explosion had not destroyed the house. He was upset that his crops were ruined, but they were easier to replace than the home. He had spent a very long time working on his house and had put great effort into the design. Steve's walls had intricate patterns that he designed with emeralds.

"What do you need for your first day of school?" asked Henry.

Lucy rattled off a list. "A diamond sword, a bow and arrow, an enchantment table, an anvil, and—"

"Wait." Henry stopped Lucy. "What do you already have?"

Lucy paused and looked through her inventory. "I think I just need a few things. Do you guys have an enchanted book?"

Steve handed Lucy an enchanted book and said, "We also have to prepare for our trip to Minecrafters Academy. Let's eat before we go on the trip."

The gang sat down and feasted on chicken and apples. They were excited to travel to the academy, but they were also worried about leaving town.

Steve remarked, "I hope there won't be any explosions while we're away."

"I'm glad I was able to destroy the spawner," said Henry. "I wouldn't have been able to leave if zombies were still roaming the village."

Max clarified, "They weren't *roaming* the village. They were attacking the village."

Lucy looked at her friends. "I'm going to miss you guys so much."

"Don't worry," Max reminded her. "You aren't getting rid of us that quickly. We still have to a few days to travel to Minecrafters Academy."

The gang finished eating, stocked their inventories with the necessary potions and other supplies, and started their trip to Minecrafters Academy. Lucy led the group. She had a detailed map that the academy had crafted.

Max studied the map with her. "It looks like we have to travel through the desert. I know we have limited time, but if we pass by any desert temples, I want to search for treasure."

"We'll see how much time we have," Lucy told Max.

The group trekked through the village. As they made their way past the village streets and into the grassy biome, Eliot approached them. "Where are you going?"

"We are traveling to Minecrafters Academy with Lucy," replied Henry.

Steve added, "Don't worry, we won't be gone too long. We want to protect this town."

"Yes," Eliot said, "I am going to need help rebuilding my shop."

"I promise we will help you rebuild when we return from our journey," Steve reassured him.

Eliot wished them well on their trip. He was sad to see them go, but he also knew they'd be back to help him rebuild the blacksmith shop.

Max led them toward the grassy biome. Cows grazed peacefully as the group made their way toward the desert. The desert temple was large and stood out in the distance.

"Can we stop in the temple for a minute?" Max asked the group. "I know we are on a tight schedule, but you never know what you might find in the temple."

As they approached the temple, Henry paused. "I think we should inspect the temple. We are making pretty good time."

Lucy looked at the map and confirmed, "We are making great time. And if we don't spend too much time in the desert temple, we will make it to the swamp before sunset. We need time to craft a home."

The group entered the desert temple.

"Ouch!" Henry grabbed his arm.

Lucy searched for the person who struck Henry, but there was nobody in sight. "They must have sprinted out of here."

Max held his diamond sword tightly as he explored the temple. "We have to be careful."

The others followed Max as they made their way toward the room where the treasure was stored. When they reached the room hidden in the lower chamber of the temple, they entered the dark room.

Lucy warned her friends, "Look, a skeleton!"

The bony beast shot an arrow at the gang and then set off a TNT explosion.

Kaboom!

The group sprinted from the explosion. Lucy looked around for her friends. She wanted to make sure they were fine and hadn't respawned in Steve's farmhouse, but she couldn't see them. Her heart began to race as she called out, "Henry! Max! Steve!"

There was no reply.

"Ouch!" she cried as an arrow pierced her skin.

Lucy spotted a skeleton in the distance. She sprinted toward the hostile mob and struck the beast with her diamond sword.

"Where are my friends?" she cried out, but the skeleton had no response. With another blow from her sword, Lucy annihilated the skeleton.

She looked around the desert temple. As she reached the exit, she began to feel very sad. She missed her friends. Lucy wanted to sprint back to the village to see if they had respawned, but she knew she had to travel to the academy. She couldn't be late. Lucy wanted the school to know that she took her role as a student very seriously. As Lucy made her way into the bright desert day, she realized that Max had the map, and she didn't know which direction she had to travel.

Chapter 4
SURVIVAL IN THE SWAMP

Lucy looked around the desert. She was nervous. "What am I going to do?" she said aloud. But there was nobody around to hear her words. Her heart raced.

"I need to focus," she told herself. She stopped pacing and stood still. It was at that moment she remembered Max mentioning that they had to travel to the swamp next. Lucy calmed down and walked in that direction. As she entered the swampy biome, a bat flew close to her head, and Lucy shouted out in terror. She hated bats. She took a deep breath and walked further into the swamp. She couldn't be scared. She had to survive. Lucy wanted to make it to school.

Lucy trekked along the murky waters of the swamp biome and kept an eye out for slimes and other hostile mobs. The sun was beginning to set, and Lucy was nervous. She needed to construct a house, but she didn't want to build it in the swamp. It was too dangerous. She sprinted through the swamp, trying to get out of there before nightfall.

Her heart skipped a beat when a witch charged toward her, clutching a potion. Before Lucy could react, the witch splashed the potion on her. Lucy stood still. She couldn't move. She cried, "Help!" But there was nobody to save her.

Lucy tried to muster up enough energy to battle the witch. She attempted to unearth a potion of strength or some milk from her inventory, but she couldn't. She was too weak.

Lucy cried out again. "Help!"

The witch had another potion and cornered Lucy. As the witch splashed the second potion on Lucy, she saw an arrow fly toward the witch. She looked to see who had shot the arrow.

"Steve!" she called out. Lucy was shocked as she watched Steve sprint toward the witch and destroy the purple-robed mob with his diamond sword.

Then Max sprinted to Lucy's side. "Are you okay?"

Henry was there, too. He handed Lucy some milk. "Take this. It will make you feel better."

"Thanks." Lucy took a sip and asked, "How did you get here?"

"We TPed," said Henry.

Steve added, "We were destroyed and respawned in my farmhouse."

Max said, "I knew that you'd probably head to the swamp, so we took a chance and TPed here to meet you."

"You guys truly saved me." Lucy was grateful for her friends.

Henry looked up at the sky. "It's going to be night soon. We should start building a house."

They sprinted out of the swamp, but before they could enter the grassy biome, Henry stopped. "Does anybody hear that sound?"

Boing! Boing! Boing!

"Oh no!" Lucy called out. "It sounds like slimes."

A group of slimes bounced toward them. Lucy tried not to fall into the swampy water as she struck one of the slimes with her diamond sword. The slime broke into smaller slimes. Henry, Steve, and Max battled the smaller slimes.

"I think we destroyed them all," Lucy called out, but as they made their way to the grassy biome, they heard more slimes bouncing toward them.

"There are more!" Henry cried.

The group tirelessly battled the remaining slimes as the sun set. It was dark now, and they were vulnerable.

"We have to get out of here!" Henry struck another slime with his sword. The gang battled the last slime, and they sprinted out of the swamp.

Lucy pointed out a spot in the grassy biome. "We can build our house here."

"Good idea!" Henry said. He picked out wooden planks from his inventory and started to lay the foundation for the house.

Lucy was happy with their progress. They were building a lot faster than she had imagined. When they were about to place the door on the house, Max shouted, "Look over there!"

A group of vacant-eyed zombies were walking toward them. Henry placed the door on the house and went inside to craft beds while his friends battled the undead mob that lurked outside of the house.

Lucy walked in the door. Max and Henry followed behind her. She looked over at the beds. "Thanks for crafting these for us."

Lucy had no energy left. She crawled into a bed and pulled the wool covers over her tired body. She fell asleep and dreamt about her first day of school. She was very excited to start at the academy.

The morning sun shone through the window. Lucy got out of bed and informed the others that she would hunt for a chicken. She was a skilled hunter and always gathered food for her friends. When Lucy returned from her hunt, she offered her friends some chicken and apples. As they feasted on breakfast, they talked about the journey.

Henry took his final bite and asked, "Should we go?"

The others followed Henry, and together, they trekked toward Minecrafters Academy. They traveled through the grassy biome and reached the mountainous biome. They climbed up a steep mountain and stopped at the peak.

Lucy pointed into the distance. "Look! You can see Minecrafters Academy from here."

The gang gathered next to Lucy. The majestic school stood out in the grassy landscape. Large trees surrounded the brick buildings, and there was a small pond on the campus. Lucy was excited. She couldn't believe she was staring at her new home. She hoped the other students at the academy were nice, and that she would be able to learn a lot while she was there.

Lucy climbed down the mountain with her friends. With each step, they were closer to Minecrafters Academy's campus. Lucy's stomach began to bother her. She was having first-day jitters.

"Are you excited, Lucy?" Henry asked.

"Yes, but I'm nervous," she confessed.

"That's normal," Max reassured Lucy. "Once you're there, you'll feel fine."

"Yes, you're going to love school," added Steve.

Lucy hoped her friends were right.

The group walked through the grassy biome and were steps from the Minecrafters Academy campus when they heard a familiar voice call out to them.

Chapter 5
FIRST DAY

Lucy turned around when she heard her name.

"Adam!" She couldn't believe her old friend was here.

"What are you doing here?" asked Steve. Adam was his old neighbor and a potion expert.

"I'm going to Minecrafters Academy," Adam replied.

"Me too!" Lucy was thrilled to know another student.

"That's great," Adam told her, "but we have to sprint. We're going to be late. Orientation starts in a couple of hours."

She knew Adam was right and they had to sprint over to the school, but she didn't want to sprint. She wanted to take her time, because she didn't want to leave Henry, Max, and Steve. She knew once school started it would be a very long time before she saw any of them. Also, Lucy was nervous for the orientation. Although the letter from the academy explained that orientation was a great place to meet other students and find out what they would be learning at the school, she didn't want to go. She wondered if the other students would like her. She wanted to tell Steve and the others that she wanted to go back to his wheat farm or on a treasure hunt with Max and Henry. She didn't want to change her entire life.

Lucy was so caught up in her thoughts, she wasn't even thinking about where she was going, which is why she was shocked when Steve said, "Look, we are at the gates of Minecrafters Academy."

Henry paused. "Wow, I can't believe we made it. I never thought I'd know anyone who got to attend this academy. And now two of my friends are going there."

Lucy took a deep breath. She wanted to be calm as she made her way through the gates and into her new life as a student at the academy.

"Welcome," said a well-dressed man in a suit. He had black hair and a very nice smile. "I work at Minecrafters Academy, I'm here to help all of the new students find their way around the school. If you have any problems when you're at school, let me know. My name is Stefan Berton. What's your name?" Stefan looked at the clipboard with all of the new student's names.

"I'm Lucy," she stuttered and stared at Stefan's clipboard.

Stefan scanned the clipboard. "Yes, Lucy. I see your name. Welcome to your new home."

Lucy's heart sunk when she heard Stefan utter those words.

She asked, "Can I have a few minutes to say good-bye to my friends?"

"Of course." Stefan smiled reassuringly at Lucy. "You're going to like it here, Lucy. I know the first day can be hard for a lot of people."

Adam stood behind Lucy. It appeared the first day wasn't going to be hard for him. He was so excited to start classes. He introduced himself to Stefan and, before Steve and the gang could say good-bye, he sprinted toward his new dorm room.

Lucy stood next to her friends. "Thank you for taking this journey to Minecrafters Academy with me. It really meant a lot to me. I am truly going to miss you guys a lot."

Steve said, "We are going to miss you, too. But this is a great opportunity for you. You'll learn so many new things. We can't wait for you to come back to the wheat farm and teach us."

Henry added, "You're going to do so well. And I'm sure you'll make a lot of new friends. By tomorrow, you'll feel like this is a new home."

Lucy hoped he was right. "Let's just make this a quick good-bye. I don't want to cry."

Steve, Henry, and Max said good-bye. Lucy turned around and saw them walking off toward the large mountain. Stefan called out to her, "Lucy, are you okay?"

"Yes," she replied, but she felt as if she was lying. She wasn't okay. She just didn't want to be a problem. She wanted the school to think she was taking her education very seriously.

Lucy walked toward her new dorm room. The dorms at the school were made of cobblestone. Lucy's dorm was called Northside. She walked into the Northside dorm and climbed three flights of stairs to her new home. She slowly opened the door to her dorm room. There were three beds with blue wool blankets, a table, and space for her crafting table and anvil.

Her two roommates were already in the room. They were decorating the room with emeralds from their inventories.

Lucy introduced herself.

"Nice to meet you, Lucy. I'm Jane." Jane wore a red shirt and jeans and had flaming red hair.

"I'm Phoebe," said a girl who wore a purple jumpsuit and had silver hair.

"It's so nice to meet both of you. Do you think we should head over to the orientation?" Lucy asked her new roommates.

"Yes, that's a good idea," replied Phoebe.

Jane looked at the information the academy had sent them. "Are we supposed to bring anything?"

"No, I don't think so." Lucy looked at the information packet, but she couldn't read it because, just then, the lights went out.

"What happened?" Phoebe asked nervously.

"I can't see anything," said Jane. She took a torch from her inventory and placed it on the wall.

The torch provided a little bit of light in the room, and Lucy spotted a spider crawling across the floor.

"A spider!" she called out.

Phoebe grabbed her diamond sword and lunged at the spider. With one strike, the spider was destroyed.

"Watch out!" Phoebe shouted.

Lucy turned around and looked at the door. Two zombies lumbered through the door. Lucy and Jane leapt at the zombies and struck them with their powerful diamond swords.

"Great job," said Phoebe. Then she asked, "Should we leave the room?"

"I'm not sure. There might be more hostile mobs lurking in the hallways." Lucy was nervous. They hadn't slept in their beds yet at the academy, which meant that if they were destroyed, they would respawn outside of the school. She feared being destroyed and having to travel back to the school alone.

"Oh no!" Jane called out.

"Ouch!" Lucy cried in pain.

Four bony skeletons walked into their dorm room and shot arrows at them. Two arrows struck Lucy.

"What are we going to do?" asked Lucy. Her energy was nearly depleted.

"Fight," Jane replied.

Chapter 6
ORIENTATION

"**O**ne skeleton down," Jane announced as she obliterated the first of the bony beasts.

"Three more to go," Phoebe gasped, leaping at one of the skeletons.

"We can do it," Lucy called to her new friends, and with another blow, she defeated a skeleton.

There were two skeletons left, but they were powerful. The beasts shot arrows at the gang. One of the arrows pierced Phoebe's arm and she cried out in pain.

"I'm losing too much energy." Phoebe sounded very nervous. Her voice shook as she explained, "I think if I'm hit one more time, I might be destroyed."

Lucy didn't have very much energy left, but she knew she had to finish the battle. She wanted to save her new friends. Lucy struck one of the skeletons, but it didn't destroy the bony mob. Phoebe and Jane were in the middle of an intense battle with the other skeleton, but they didn't seem to be winning. Lucy was worried. She didn't want anyone being destroyed. Her heart was racing. She struck the skeleton again, but it was still fighting back. Another arrow struck her arm and Lucy knew she didn't have any strength left. She looked over at Phoebe. Phoebe was underneath the table and drinking some milk. The table shielded her from the arrows.

"I'm also low on energy," Lucy called out to Phoebe.

"I have some milk for you." Phoebe dodged arrows as she tried to bring the milk over to Lucy.

It was impossible to bring milk to Lucy in the middle of the battle. Phoebe put the milk back in her inventory and took out a diamond sword. She struck the skeleton and it was destroyed.

"Thank you!" Lucy was relieved.

"Here." Phoebe handed the milk to Lucy.

Jane defeated the final skeleton and Lucy offered her some of Phoebe's milk. As they drank the milk, their energy was restored.

"We did it!" Jane exclaimed after taking a sip of the milk.

"Yes!" Lucy was excited, but her heart beat rapidly when she saw a horde of zombies enter their room.

"It's never ending!" Jane used her renewed strength to leap at the zombies and quickly destroyed a couple.

Phoebe and Lucy battled the zombies, but were relieved when the lights came back on and the zombies disappeared.

Lucy looked around the room and asked her friends, "Do you think that was a test?"

Phoebe was confused. "You mean, you think that attack was a part of our training?"

"I'm not sure. It just seems so random. I mean, we were heading to orientation and then the lights went out." Lucy couldn't make sense of the attack.

"You could be right," Jane said as they walked out the door and to their orientation meeting. "Maybe they wanted to see who would survive. It could be a test."

"If that's true, it's pretty awful," remarked Phoebe. "I wouldn't want to attend a school that invites you to be a student and then asks you to leave if you can't survive a surprise attack on the very first day."

Lucy agreed with Phoebe. She hoped they wouldn't find out it was a test when they entered the orientation.

The trio entered a large room with wood-paneled walls. They stood by a wooden bench. The room was crowded with new students. Lucy saw Adam, and she looked around to see if she recognized anyone else in the crowd, but she didn't.

Stefan stood at a podium. "Welcome, new students. I want to apologize for the power outage. We never lose lights in the middle of the day, and I hope it doesn't happen again. Many of you told me that you were attacked by hostile mobs. My sincerest apologies. I would never want any new student injured or destroyed while at Minecrafters Academy. Yes, you might be destroyed while in a class as you learn new techniques, but you will respawn in your dorm room. But the attacks that took place today were unique. We have never experienced anything like this at Minecrafters Academy."

Lucy wondered if griefers were attacking the school. Maybe there were students that didn't get accepted and they wanted to destroy the school. But she didn't want to let her mind wander with different theories. She had to pay attention. This was the first day, and she was going to find out a lot of important information.

Stefan continued, "I hope everyone likes their living quarters and has spent some time getting to know their new roommates."

Lucy hadn't spent much time with her roommates, but she knew she could rely on them in a battle, and that was a very important thing to know. It didn't matter where they came from or what they had done before Minecrafters Academy. Although she was curious to know their stories, she was just happy that she had two people she could trust sharing a room with her.

Stefan introduced the head of the school. "I'd like everyone to meet Headmaster Isaac."

Isaac walked up to the podium and thanked Stefan. Isaac wore a red robe and a monocle.

"I want to tell you all how happy I am that you are attending this school. The academics here are extremely rigorous. But you will learn a lot. Each day we will study another facet of the Minecraft universe. When you graduate, you will be a potion expert, a master builder, and a skilled fighter. Tomorrow is your first day of classes. Get some rest now. Be sure to sleep in your beds and never sleep off campus. It's important that you always respawn in your dorm room. This will make learning at the academy a great place to experiment. It doesn't matter what happens to you here, because you will always respawn in your bed."

Lucy felt better after the orientation. She was excited to learn about the Minecraft universe and master many skills she'd be scared to learn when she was in the Overworld. Knowing that she would be able to respawn in her dorm room made her feel secure.

Lucy walked back to the dorm with her new friends. It was dinnertime, and the gang settled in the large dining hall in their dorm. They all took trays and gathered food from a buffet. Lucy took chicken, apples, and a large piece of cake.

Lucy saw Adam eating his dinner and walked over to him.

"What did you think of the orientation?" Lucy asked him.

"It was hard to pay attention. I was exhausted from the zombie battle before the orientation meeting. My roommates and I were battling a zombie invasion," Adam replied and then took a bite of his chicken.

"We were also attacked by zombies," said Lucy.

"I have a feeling something is happening at this school that the headmaster and Stefan aren't telling us about." Adam took another bite of his chicken.

"They told us that was a rare occurrence. And any time the lights go out, hostile mobs can respawn."

Adam nodded. "But I still think something isn't right."

"I hope not," said Lucy, and she walked back to her friends.

As she reached the table, the lights went out again.

Chapter 7
BREWING 101

"Watch out!" Phoebe called to Lucy.

A zombie was lurking behind Lucy. Lucy leapt at the undead zombie with her diamond sword.

A shrill scream echoed through the hall.

"Is everyone okay?" Jane asked the other students eating in the dining hall. She grabbed a torch and placed it on the wall.

"Everyone, take out your torches," instructed Phoebe.

All the students took out their torches and placed them on the wall. They created enough light with the torches to ward off the zombies. In a few minutes, the light came back on.

Stefan entered the dining hall and announced, "I'm sorry for these blackouts. Please go on and finish your dinner. You need your strength. If we have another blackout, we might have to battle more zombies and skeletons."

A student raised his hand. "Why is this happening?"

Stefan replied, "We don't know."

Another student raised their hand. "Does the school have any enemies?"

Stefan paused. "No, but that's a good question. Isaac and I will go over the list of students who graduated and became griefers. It's a very short list. We pride ourselves on educating people who make the Overworld a better place. But every now and then, we get a student who wants to use their power for evil. I don't like to admit it, but we do have some noted evil alumni."

Lucy wondered what evil griefers had attended Minecrafters Academy. She also wondered if something had happened while they were attending the school that might have made them turn into griefers.

Phoebe looked over at her new friends. "I think we should head straight to bed after dinner. I don't want to risk respawning in one of the biomes I traveled through on my way to the school."

Jane and Lucy agreed. But before they could finish dinner and leave the table, another blackout occurred. Zombies filled the room instantly.

All of the students began to battle the zombies.

Adam called out to Lucy, "I bet there is a spawner on campus!"

Lucy and Adam broke away from the group and explored the building. Adam said, "I thought I saw a staircase to a basement when I was heading into the dining hall."

Lucy and Adam searched for the staircase, but it was too dark, and they couldn't see. Lucy didn't have a torch in her inventory. "Adam, do you have a torch?"

"No, I used them all during the attacks." Adam unearthed a bottle from his inventory. "But I do have this."

Adam handed her a night vision potion. Lucy took a sip and was able to spot a group of zombies headed in their direction. They took out their diamond swords and battled the zombies. Within seconds, the undead mob was destroyed. Adam sprinted down the hall and Lucy followed.

Lucy stopped. "Adam, I see it! I see the staircase."

The duo was about to walk down the staircase when the lights went back on. Adam wanted to continue on to explore the basement, but Lucy said, "I think I should head back to my room and sleep. I don't want to respawn off-campus."

Adam nodded. "I have to wake up early, too. I have a brewing class in the morning."

"I also have a brewing class," said Lucy.

"I'll see you there," Adam said and then added, "I'm glad I ran into you. It's good to know someone here. Someone I trust. Also, we've been through so much together after Thomas invaded Steve's town."

Lucy remembered their intense battle with Thomas. "I feel the same way. But I'm not going to let these attacks ruin my experience at Minecrafters Academy. I will work hard and learn. This won't distract me."

"Me, too," Adam agreed, and they went their separate ways.

Lucy entered her dorm room and Phoebe sprinted to the door. "Lucy! It's so good to see you. We were very worried about you."

Jane said, "I was so upset. Phoebe and I thought you respawned at another spot. We were devastated."

Phoebe said, "Well, I'm glad to see you're here now. We should get to bed. We have classes early in the morning."

Lucy explained, "I'm sorry that I scared you. I saw my old friend Adam and we started to search for a zombie spawner."

"Do you think a griefer spawned the zombies?" Phoebe asked.

"I'm not sure, but there were too many zombies for this to be a natural occurrence," Lucy said.

Jane agreed. "I think this could be the work of a griefer. If we discover who the griefer is, maybe we'll graduate head of the class!"

Phoebe was shocked. "This isn't about us getting ahead. We want to do this because we want to help the school."

Lucy climbed into bed. "I think we should just try and solve this mystery, but I also believe we have to get some sleep. It's too risky not to go to bed. I want to know that we will all respawn together."

The roommates agreed. They fell asleep. When they awoke, Lucy felt less anxious. She had made it through her first day, and she knew that no matter what happened today, she would respawn in her dorm room with her new friends.

The trio went to the dining hall for breakfast. Lucy was excited because the school offered them cake at every meal.

Phoebe took a bite of the cake and asked her new friends about their schedules. Lucy told them she had to go to brewing class.

"I also have to go there," said Jane.

"Me too!" Phoebe exclaimed. She was happy that she had friends in her first class.

The three friends walked into the classroom together. The teacher wore a green robe. She stood in front of the class and held a vial.

"Welcome to brewing class," the teacher said. Then she splashed a potion on the class and everyone disappeared.

"Your first challenge is to make yourself reappear," the teacher instructed the class.

Adam was the first in the class to reappear. Lucy wasn't surprised. It took her longer to reappear. She was one of the last students to complete the task. But she had never been very good with potions. Lucy was a skilled hunter and that was why she had been asked to attend the school. She was excited to learn a lot about potions and become a potion expert, too.

The teacher helped Lucy brew potions to gain strength. Lucy listened, but was distracted when she heard someone talking in the hallway. It sounded like the headmaster, and she thought he was talking about a zombie spawner.

Chapter 8
NOW OR NETHER

Lucy wasn't certain the headmaster was talking about the zombie spawner. She wasn't even sure the voice she heard was the headmaster's voice. So she decided not to mention it to her friends. Instead, she kept a close eye on the headmaster and listened carefully to anyone who might be talking about the zombie invasion. She wanted to end the invasion, so she could concentrate on her studies. At lunchtime, Lucy made the strategic decision to sit near the staff. The faculty usually sat at their own table. Lucy chose a table next to them, so she could overhear their conversations.

Phoebe sprinted over to Lucy. "Can I eat with you?"

"Yes," said Lucy, but really, she wanted to be alone. This was the best time to eavesdrop on the faculty.

Jane sprinted over and joined them. "Did you hear the news?"

"What news?" Lucy wondered if it was about the zombie spawner. Stopping the zombie invasion was all she could think about.

"We are all going to the Nether after lunch," announced Jane.

"Really? How do you know?" asked Lucy.

Phoebe explained, "I was talking to Stefan about the zombie invasion."

"What were you talking about? What did he say?" Lucy interrupted.

"I just told him that these attacks were making me nervous and I wondered what they were doing to find out who was behind them."

"And? What did he say?" Lucy asked.

Jane explained, "He said that they didn't know. He also mentioned there would be a big general meeting about it with the entire school after we come back from the Nether. Then I asked about the Nether, and he told me that it was an outing that they always do on the first day of classes. We will learn to battle and also how to pick up valuable resources for brewing potions."

"That sounds like fun," said Phoebe.

"Fun? The Nether?" Lucy was shocked. She disliked the Nether. Although she had discovered many treasures in Nether fortresses, she disliked battling ghasts, blazes, and other fiery mobs that spawned in the crimson biome.

"I don't like the Nether, either," said Jane, "but I'm excited to learn how to survive in the Nether. I've always had such bad luck in the Nether. Once, I drowned in lava."

"Yes, I've had bad experiences there, too," Lucy told her.

"I've never been there," Phoebe announced.

"Wow, really?" Lucy was surprised, but now she understood why Phoebe was excited to travel to the deadly biome.

"Where are you from?" asked Jane. "I find it hard to believe you've never been to the Nether."

Phoebe replied, "I live in a grassy biome, but I am usually on Creative mode and I just build structures. People come from all around the Overworld to see my creations. I've built bridges and houses."

"That sounds like fun," Lucy said. "But you have to be very careful in the Nether. Mobs spawn in the sky and shoot fireballs at you."

"Don't scare her," Jane said to Lucy.

"I'm not trying to scare her. I just want to prepare her. It's not a fun field trip. It's serious. She has to use this opportunity to learn a lot about the hostile environment."

Jane looked at Phoebe. "Stick with me. I'll stay close by and protect you during the trip to the Nether."

"I'll do the same," Lucy said. She felt bad for scaring Phoebe. She had thought she was just being helpful.

Isaac, the headmaster, stood up and made an announcement at lunch. "After we finish eating, we will all meet outside and craft portals to the Nether. This is a very important day for the academy. This is a day where we learn survival skills that we will use throughout our time at Minecrafters Academy. Pay attention when you're in the Nether."

The trio exited and walked outside the dorm. Groups of people were working together to craft portals to the Nether. Stefan walked over to them. "Everyone must enter the Nether with a leader." He looked down at his clipboard. "You're in the group with Eitan. He will be your teacher."

The gang was excited as Stefan led them over to their teacher.

Eitan instructed his students, "We have to watch out for each other. When we get to the Nether, I will teach you the best way to battle a ghast and other hostile mobs. I will also have you look for resources to brew powerful potions."

Phoebe confessed, "I've never been to the Nether and I'm really scared."

Eitan told her, "I've taken many people to the Nether for their first time and they've done very well. They are especially alert because they are in an unfamiliar territory. Some people who have been there many times are too confident and think they know everything. Those are the people that I'm worried about. They can get very hurt during a trip to the Nether."

Eitan taught them how to craft a portal out of obsidian, and within seconds, a purple mist surrounded them and they were in the middle of the Nether.

"Watch out!" Lucy warned Phoebe.

Three ghasts flew toward them and unleashed fiery blasts at the gang.

Eitan instructed them, "No weapons. Just punch the fireball and aim it back in their direction."

Phoebe was frozen. She had never seen a ghast, and the fireball was heading straight toward her. She didn't want to touch it, because she was afraid she'd get burned or destroyed. Phoebe sprinted from the fireball and it landed on the netherrack ground.

Lucy used her fist, and with a powerful blow, she hit the fireball and it flew toward the ghast.

Kaboom!

The ghast was destroyed.

"Good job," Eitan cheered.

Jane also used her fist to defeat a ghast.

"Excellent!" Eitan was proud of his new students.

The remaining ghast shot more fireballs. As Jane prepared to strike the next fireball, Eitan called out, "No. Let Phoebe do it."

"No, Jane can destroy it." Phoebe's voice shook.

"You can't run away. You have to face your fears. Punch the fireball and destroy the ghast," Eitan told her.

"No, I don't even want to be here. I'm not a fighter. I'm a builder," Phoebe protested. "I want to live on Creative mode."

"If you want to advance yourself, you have to take chances. To be an expert, you have to learn to survive on all the settings." Eitan's voice grew louder.

Jane and Lucy dodged the fireballs. Both of them wanted to destroy the ghast, but they knew Eitan would be upset, and they also knew that Phoebe had to learn to get over her fears of the Nether. Lucy really understood. She was terrified during her first trip to the Nether, but her friends Henry and Max wouldn't let her give up.

They had told her that once she found the treasure in the Nether fortress, the trip would be worth the fear and hassle. Lucy remembered opening her first treasure chest deep within the Nether fortress. She had been so excited to discover the treasure that she had realized traveling to the Nether wasn't as bad as she had originally thought. But she couldn't explain this to Phoebe. Phoebe had to discover it on her own.

"The fireball is headed in your direction. You must strike it, Phoebe," Eitan informed his petrified student.

Lucy called out, "Phoebe, if you get destroyed, you'll respawn in your bed and will be out of the Nether. That's the worst that can happen."

Eitan looked over at Lucy. He was the teacher and he didn't want Lucy taking over his role.

Phoebe sprinted forward and struck the flaming ball. It flew toward the ghast.

Kaboom!

The ghast exploded.

"You did it!" Jane was so happy for her friend.

Eitan walked over to Lucy. "I'm glad you encouraged your friend. You did a good job."

"Thanks," Lucy replied. "I'm glad you feel that way. I didn't want to overstep my boundaries."

"No, it's good that you guys work together as a team and get each other to take chances. I see you already trust each other. That is a hard thing to teach, and your relationship with each other makes my job a lot easier. I am here to teach you skills. You have to learn to build relationships."

Lucy was happy that Eitan was pleased with her work. "I think Jane, Phoebe, and I have become friends quite quickly."

Jane and Phoebe agreed.

"Good," Eitan said. "Let's travel further into the Nether. We have a lot of exploring to do."

Lucy and the gang walked along a lava stream. They watched for ghasts, blazes, and other hostile mobs that spawned in this fiery biome. Lucy spotted the headmaster and some of the other faculty members enter a Nether fortress in the distance. She wanted to sprint toward them to hear what they were talking about during their trip to the Nether.

"A Nether fortress," Lucy exclaimed. She asked Eitan, "Can we search for treasure?"

"I'm sure it's been emptied, but I will teach you how to search for valuable resources for various potions. And I will also teach you how to battle magma cubes," Eitan said, and then led his team toward the Nether fortress.

Four blazes flew high above the entrance to the Nether fortress.

"What should we do?" Phoebe asked nervously.

"Get out your bow and arrows," Eitan instructed them.

The gang shot arrows at the blazes.

"I got one!" Lucy called out when she destroyed a blaze.

"Me too!" exclaimed Jane.

"You can do it, Phoebe." Eitan watched as Phoebe nervously aimed at the blaze.

"I destroyed it!" Phoebe was both shocked and thrilled.

Eitan said, "Okay, you did a good job, Phoebe. But I want you to destroy the last blaze."

"I have to destroy another one?" she asked, taking a deep breath.

"Yes, I want this to become routine. I don't want you to think about destroying the blazes. Having control in the Nether is the only way you can survive. If you panic every time you see a blaze, you will lose the game. Now, destroy it."

Phoebe listened to Eitan's words and aimed at the blaze. With one hit from her arrow, the blaze was destroyed.

"That was fantastic. Now, you get to enter the Nether fortress first," Eitan told her.

"First?" Phoebe asked Eitan, "But what if a magma cube attacks me?"

"Then you'll take out your diamond sword and you will attack it." Eitan added, "And we'll be right behind you, and will help you battle the smaller cubes."

Phoebe walked into the fortress, clutching her diamond sword. She was nervous. As she entered the main room, she calmed down. She didn't spot any hostile mobs.

Lucy could hear people speaking in the other room. As Eitan lectured them about the importance of Nether wart and potions, Lucy walked off and tried to eavesdrop on the conversation that was taking place in the other room. She walked down the hall and peeked in the room. She spotted Headmaster Isaac talking to three people she had never seen before. They were three men dressed in blue suits.

"I will take over the Minecraft Universe," Isaac told the men in the blue suits.

Lucy almost gasped, but she knew she had to remain quiet and still. She didn't want anyone seeing her. She tried to hide behind the door.

"Yes, we will help you. What else do you want us to do?" asked one of the men dressed in a blue suit.

"I want you to increase the amount of zombie attacks," Isaac told them.

"What about spawning more hostile mobs?" asked one of the men.

Another man asked, "Can we spawn the Ender Dragon?"

"No," Isaac answered. "We want to make this attack look as if it might be a natural occurrence or a glitch."

"Okay, just tell us what you want us to do and we'll do it," one of the men told him.

"Tonight we must stage something at the big meeting. We have lots of students there, and we must show them we are in control."

"What do you have in mind?" one of the men asked.

"Well, I was thinking that in the middle of the meeting we could have—" Isaac's voice was cut off as Lucy heard Eitan calling for her.

"Lucy!" Eitan sounded annoyed. Lucy wanted to listen to Isaac talk about his plans. She had to make a decision. She had to decide if she should listen or leave.

As Eitan's calls grew louder, she feared that Isaac would discover her, and she sprinted toward Eitan.

"Don't wander off." Eitan was upset with Lucy. "I was in the middle of teaching you about Nether wart."

"I'm sorry. I was just so excited to be inside the Nether fortress and I started to look around."

"You can't do things like that. We have to stick together." Eitan continued to lecture Lucy on the importance of following the rules.

Lucy stood silently and listened. She wanted to explain what had happened and how the headmaster was planning taking over the Overworld, but she didn't say anything except, "I'm sorry. I'll never do it again." She wasn't sure who she could trust.

"Okay," Eitan said. "Just don't do it again. We've lost a lot of time talking about this, and I have a lot to teach you."

Headmaster Isaac walked into the main room. He was alone. The men in blue suits must have vanished. Lucy wondered where they were. She assumed that they had taken a potion of invisibility and were possibly walking past the gang at that very moment, but she wasn't sure.

Eitan looked shocked to see the headmaster. "Headmaster, how nice to see you in the Nether fortress. I was just teaching my students about the importance of Nether wart when brewing potions."

"Good job," Isaac said as he walked out of the Nether fortress.

Lucy wanted to shout at the headmaster. She wanted him to know that she knew his secrets, but she kept quiet and listened to Eitan talk about Nether wart.

Boing! Boing!

"Did you hear that noise?" Phoebe asked nervously.

"That's a magma cube," Eitan said calmly. "I'll teach you how to battle them."

Everyone took out their diamond swords.

"Over there!" Lucy shouted.

"I know you can battle these cubes easily. You guys know how to work together and trust each other," Eitan said, and then he watched his students destroy the slimy beasts.

Lucy thought about her new friends and how they would react to her news about the headmaster. She was able to trust them as they played these games in class, but she wondered how trustworthy they would be in a real battle.

Chapter 9:
SECRETS AND LIES

Purple mist enveloped them as they made their way back to the Overworld.

"That was an amazing trip," Phoebe said as she walked off the portal.

"I'm glad you enjoyed your first trip to the Nether. There is a lot more to learn about the Nether, and that is only the first of many trips we will take during your time at Minecrafters Academy," Eitan explained.

"I'm excited to learn all about the Nether," Phoebe told her teacher.

"Great. Now it's time for us to eat dinner and then we all have to attend a meeting about the blackouts," said Eitan.

Lucy started to panic. She wanted to tell her friends about the attack Isaac was planning at the meeting. As they walked toward the dining hall, Lucy burst out, "Isaac is evil!"

"What are you talking about?" asked Phoebe.

"Have you lost your mind?" Jane was upset. "He's the headmaster. He's also the one who chose us and invited us to study here. He isn't a bad guy."

"But I overheard him talking to three men dressed in blue suits at the Nether fortress. They were helping him plot an attack on the school," Lucy blurted out.

"That's not true," said Phoebe.

Jane added, "When we saw Isaac in the Nether fortress, he was alone. I didn't see any men in blue suits."

"They must have taken a potion of invisibility or something, but I'm telling you that I overheard Isaac, and he has plans to take over the Minecraft Universe. He is a griefer," Lucy explained, but she could tell her friends didn't believe her. She had thought they trusted her, but she also knew that they had just met. They really didn't know Lucy.

"Isaac. A griefer? Now, that is the silliest thing I've ever heard." Phoebe looked at Lucy in disbelief.

"But it's true. I wish you'd believe me," Lucy pleaded.

"I don't want to hear anymore of this nonsense." Jane was upset with Lucy. "I just want to eat my dinner and go to the meeting."

Lucy walked behind her two friends. When they entered the dining hall, Phoebe and Jane went off and left Lucy. Lucy felt very sad. She regretted telling her new friends about Isaac's plan. She also began to wonder if she hadn't heard Isaac properly. Maybe he was talking to those men to help stop the attacks. But Lucy was sure she had heard him right. Isaac was a griefer. Isaac was going to attack the school and was plotting to take over the Overworld. Isaac had to be stopped. She might have lost her two new friends, but she knew that there was one person at Minecrafters Academy that would believe her. She had to find Adam.

Lucy grabbed a tray and filled it with chicken, potatoes, and other food. All the while, her eyes searched for Adam in the dining hall. She looked all around the room, but she didn't see him. Lucy carried her tray around the room, but he was nowhere in sight. Lucy was worried that something had happened to her friend. She began to wonder, and her head filled with scary thoughts. Maybe he was also suspicious of Isaac and was destroyed? She couldn't think this way. Adam could be in his room— or maybe he finished his dinner before her. Lucy took her tray over to the table closest to the faculty. Now that she had no friends, she wouldn't be distracted when she wanted to eavesdrop on Isaac.

"We have to eat quickly and get our energy up," Lucy heard Isaac say to the other staff members. "We have the meeting soon, and we want to be prepared. There is a possibility that the school is under attack and we have to stop it."

"Do you think it's seriously under attack?" one of the teachers asked Isaac.

Isaac paused. "I'm not sure. But I don't want another blackout or another zombie invasion. We must do something to stop it."

"Why would someone want to attack the school?" asked another teacher.

"We are a school filled with the most elite Minecraft players. Can't you see why we are a target?" he replied.

"I guess so," one of the teachers said, "but I also thought we would be strong enough to stop any attack."

"Yes, why would someone attack us? We are too strong," added another teacher.

"I guess they are testing our power and our egos." Isaac looked over at the teachers.

Lucy wondered what was motivating Isaac to try to destroy the school and to take over the Minecraft Universe. He must have a large ego and crave power, but could there be something even more sinister?

Lucy listened to the conversation between the faculty members, but there wasn't anything important being discussed. They were all chatting about the meeting and their food. She wanted more information. She wanted to run over to the table and confront Isaac. Instead, she scanned the dining hall for Adam, but she didn't see him anywhere.

Isaac raised his voice and announced, "We should all finish our food and head to the main meeting hall. We must discuss the blackout."

The minute Isaac said the word blackout, the dining hall went dark and zombies filled the room.

"Help!" a voice called out. Cries filled the room.

Lucy grabbed her diamond sword and began to strike as many vacant-eyed zombies as she could hit.

The students of Minecrafters Academy were involved in a serious battle against the zombies. Lucy watched several students being destroyed. Three zombies surrounded her. She fought back, but soon she was losing energy. Lucy knew that she was losing the battle and she would be destroyed. She was about to use her last bit of energy to strike a zombie, when Adam came up behind her and splashed a potion on the zombies and struck them with his diamond sword.

"Take this." He handed Lucy a potion to regain her strength.

"I have something important to tell you," Lucy said as she battled zombies.

"I think we have to concentrate on this battle," Adam called back. He was busy destroying zombies. This was a tireless battle.

Without warning, the lights turned on again. Isaac stood on a table and announced, "I'm sorry for that blackout and zombie attack. It appears someone must be targeting our school. I believe there have been too many zombies and too many blackouts for this to be a coincidence."

Lucy looked at Isaac. It took a lot of willpower not to shout at him and announce that he was a griefer.

Adam looked over at Lucy and said, "I don't trust Isaac."

Lucy smiled. She had someone she could trust. Maybe there was hope after all.

Chapter 10
BIG BATTLES

Adam stood next to Lucy during the meeting about the blackout. Everyone was quiet as they listened to Isaac talk about the attacks. Lucy's heart was beating fast. She was certain that Isaac had been planning something, but she didn't know what he had on the agenda. She looked over at Adam. She had told him briefly about what she heard Isaac discussing with the men in blue suits.

Adam looked at Lucy. "When do you think he is going to attack?"

"I'm not sure," Lucy replied. "I left too soon. Maybe he called off the attack. Maybe it already happened in the dining hall."

"No, that was a very small-scale attack. I bet he is planning something much bigger."

"You're probably right, Adam." Lucy was scared. She didn't want another attack. She wanted to go back to her room and talk to her roommates. She was still upset that they hadn't believed her when she had told them about Isaac.

"We need to be prepared," Isaac called out. "I dislike telling students to think about something other than their studies when they are at Minecrafters Academy, but we need to be on the lookout for other attacks. We need to always have our diamond swords ready for battle. But remember that we are still on Survival mode, so if you are destroyed during one of these attacks, you will respawn."

Lucy hoped Isaac didn't plan on changing their settings to Hardcore with command blocks. She didn't trust him at all. Adam kept looking over at her. He was wondering when the major attack would take place. She was wondering, too. But she continued to listen to Isaac's speech.

At the podium, he said, "This is just something that will distract us for awhile, but it will not stop us from learning. We will conquer this enemy."

Lucy wanted to shout out that Isaac was the enemy, but when the meeting ended and there was no attack, she began to question herself.

Phoebe and Jane walked over to Lucy. Phoebe said, "I guess you were wrong. There wasn't a big battle at the meeting."

"I know, but I heard him talking about the battle with the men in blue suits," Lucy defended herself.

Lucy was shocked when Adam turned to her and said, "You have to get your facts right. This is serious. You can't accuse someone of being a griefer."

"But you said you didn't trust him!" Lucy looked at Adam.

"I do now," Adam said to Lucy. "After listening to Isaac talk to us about the school and how strong we are, I realize that we are in this together. Maybe you heard Isaac talking about getting help to end the attack when you were in the Nether fortress. Maybe they were protectors of the Overworld, *not* criminals?"

Phoebe and Jane agreed with Adam. Jane said, "You have to admit that what you're saying sounds really crazy."

"But I overheard him talking. He was plotting to take over the Overworld," Lucy pleaded with her friends. She watched Adam side with Phoebe and Jane, and Lucy felt very alone. She had lost one of her closest and oldest friends, and she had also alienated her two new friends and roommates. Phoebe and Jane were her partners at school, and if they didn't trust each other, she would be very isolated during her time at the academy.

The room had emptied out, but the four of them remained. Stefan walked over to the group. "Is everything okay?" Stefan asked them.

"Yes," Lucy replied. "I'm just very worried about the attacks and my friends are trying to comfort me."

"Yes, I can see a lot of people are worried. I wish I could tell you that the attacks would end soon, but I know as much as you do. The attacks are just a nuisance. They won't destroy this school. We have a fantastic and trustworthy headmaster, and we must follow him."

"I know. You're right," Lucy replied, but she wasn't sure she was telling the truth.

Chapter 11
LOST FRIENDS

Lucy felt very alone. She walked back to the dorm room and held her head down when she entered her room. Phoebe and Jane were in their beds. Lucy climbed into her bed and pulled her wool cover over herself. She wanted to disappear. Her friends must have noticed, because Phoebe said, "I want to apologize for being mean. I know you thought you heard Isaac talk about attacking the school. But you have to admit that you were wrong."

Lucy could have just replied that she was wrong and misheard Isaac, but she didn't want to lie. Before she could respond, they heard a loud explosion.

"What's that?" Phoebe leapt out of bed and sprinted toward the window.

Jane, too, sprinted to the window and stood beside Phoebe. Lucy stayed in bed. She wasn't sure what she should do.

"Oh no!" Jane looked out the window. "It looks like one of the classroom buildings was blown up."

There was a knock at their door.

"I'm too scared to answer it," confessed Phoebe.

Jane stood next to Phoebe and continued to stare out the window. Lucy got out of bed and opened the door.

"Hi." Stefan stood at the door. "There was an explosion in a classroom. Someone has placed TNT around the campus and we don't know when they are going to activate it. We need all students on campus to search for TNT. We aren't safe here."

"But it's dark out. We can be attacked by naturally spawned hostile mobs." Phoebe was scared. She didn't want to search for TNT. She wanted to stay in the room.

"I know. We have placed as many torches around the campus as we could, but there is nothing we can do about it. It's not safe to stay here. If these dorms explode, you will have no place to respawn."

Phoebe began to pace the room and panic. "Then where we will we respawn?"

"It's going to be okay," Lucy comforted her as they walked into the hall and exited the building to search for TNT.

Lucy spotted Adam in the dark. He was searching around the dorms. She called his name.

"Lucy!" Adam walked over to her. "We need to find the TNT."

Just then, Lucy looked down and spotted a brick of TNT.

Stefan walked over with Isaac. Isaac saw the TNT in Lucy's hand and asked, "Who found that?"

Lucy stood silently. She wanted to confront Stefan, but instead she said nothing. Adam responded, "She did. Lucy found the TNT."

Isaac looked at Lucy. "That was a great find. We need more students like you on campus. We must find all of this TNT tonight or we'll never be safe."

Lucy didn't respond. She didn't even warn Isaac when she saw a green creeper silently creep up behind him.

Kaboom!

Isaac was destroyed. Stefan shouted, "Oh no! Isaac!"

"But it doesn't matter if we're destroyed. We just respawn in our beds," Lucy said to Stefan.

"Please, Lucy, don't be disrespectful. How can you say that about our beloved headmaster? He was destroyed by a creeper."

Adam shot Lucy a dirty look. Lucy covered up her anger. "I'm sorry. I just said that because I was nervous. It's hard to see someone so powerful destroyed."

"It's okay, Lucy," Stefan told her. "I need to make sure Isaac is okay."

As Stefan sprinted off toward the faculty housing, Lucy and Adam continued their search for the TNT.

"Lucy, I feel like this attack on the school has been especially hard on you. Maybe you should take some time off from school and go visit Steve on the wheat farm."

Lucy was shocked that Adam suggested that she return to the wheat farm. "What? Leave school? Go back to the wheat farm?"

"Yes. Maybe you need a break." Adam looked at the ground and noticed a brick of TNT. He called out, "I found another brick."

A group of school officials sprinted over to Adam and collected the brick. Lucy asked the school officials, "Have you found a lot of TNT?"

"Yes," one of the officials replied, "I don't think we will have to search much longer. Soon we can all get back to sleep."

Lucy wished the TNT hunt was over and she was in bed, but that wasn't the case. She was stunned when Adam shouted, "Watch out, Lucy. There's a spider jockey!"

Lucy shot an arrow at the skeleton and Adam attacked the spider. With their last bits of strength, a diamond sword, potions, and skill, they were able to defeat the spider jockey.

"See, we still make a good team," Lucy said.

"I know, but I worry about you and your idea about Isaac being a griefer."

"I'll trust him. I have to. He's our leader." Lucy resigned herself to this belief. There was no hope of anyone believing her.

A few moments later, Stefan announced that they could go back to their dorm rooms. Lucy and Adam walked back to their rooms, but stopped when they heard a familiar voice call out their names.

"Can that be?" Lucy looked at Adam.

"We have to find out," Adam said as they walked in the direction of the voices.

Chapter 12
HOME AGAIN

"Henry, what are you doing here?" Lucy was surprised to see her friend on the campus.

"We need help," Henry whispered. "The town is under attack by zombies!"

"That's also happening here," Adam told Henry.

"I know. Your headmaster, Isaac, is behind it. He has an army of men in blue suits spotted around town at night. They blow up various buildings with TNT." Henry spoke quickly.

"How do you know it's Isaac?" asked Adam.

"Everyone in the Overworld knows. He has staged an attack on the Overworld. I assume you don't know because you are isolated on this campus and he is controlling it," explained Henry.

Adam looked over at Lucy. "I'm sorry I didn't believe you."

"It's okay," Lucy replied. All that mattered was that they were on the same team now.

Lucy asked Henry, "Are you alone? Where are the others?"

"Steve is back at the wheat farm. I have Max with me, but he was hiding by the entrance. He is supposed to warn me if Isaac is close by."

"Isaac was destroyed by a creeper. He probably respawned and will be coming back out here. We should go quickly," Lucy told Henry.

Adam was nervous. "Can we just leave?"

Lucy replied, "Of course. We are at a school being led by a griefer. We can do whatever we want."

"We have to go now! Look!" Henry was staring at a horde of zombies that were heading in their direction.

Stefan sprinted into the center of the campus and shouted, "Zombie attack! Zombie attack! We need all students to help!"

All the students rushed into the center of the campus and battled the zombies.

Henry looked over at Adam and Lucy. "This is our chance. We have to make our escape now."

The trio sprinted through the campus and toward Max, who was standing by the gate.

"Max!" Lucy called out.

The group began to sprint through the gate when Stefan called out, "Come back!"

They didn't turn around. They sprinted through the night, trying to avoid hostile mobs. They were making great time until they reached the swamp biome. It was there that a witch sprinted out of her hut and splashed a potion on them.

Adam and Henry were immediately frozen and weak. Lucy had barely enough strength to pull some milk from her inventory. She sipped some milk and handed it to her friends. As her friends drank the milk, Lucy sprinted toward the witch and struck the witch with her powerful diamond sword.

Adam and Max joined Lucy, and they struck the witch with their diamond swords. When the witch was destroyed, they continued to sprint until they reached the village. They looked at Eliot's shop. It was still destroyed.

"We're almost at the wheat farm." Lucy was excited.

"Help!" they heard Steve call out.

The gang sprinted toward his house. A large group of zombies were surrounding Steve.

The gang rushed toward the group of zombies and attacked them. Lucy struck a zombie with her diamond sword, but two zombies clobbered her. She realized that she was running low on energy. She tried to fight, but a blow from a zombie destroyed her.

"Lucy." Phoebe was staring at her.

"Where were you?" Jane asked.

"Where am I?" Lucy was confused.

"You're in your dorm room. And you just missed Stefan. He came in here and informed us that you ran away. We were worried. There are people searching for you all over the Overworld," Jane explained.

"What? Why?"

"You need to drink something. You don't seem well." Phoebe took out some milk from her inventory and handed it to Lucy.

"And you need to eat." Jane gave Lucy a piece of chicken.

Lucy ate the chicken and drank the milk, and thanked her friends. "I'm sorry that I worried you guys. And I want to tell you something, but I don't think you're going to believe me."

"You're not going to start in on Isaac again. We told you that we don't want to talk about that anymore," Jane protested.

"This is serious." Lucy took another sip of milk.

"Oh, my!" Phoebe exclaimed, as Adam, Henry, and Max appeared in the dorm room.

"How did you get here?" asked Jane.

"We TPed. We need Lucy. This is very important." Henry told them.

Jane looked at Henry. "I don't know who you are, but Lucy isn't well and she needs to stay here. Also, everyone on campus was worried about her and they have a search team looking for her in the Overworld. We must inform Stefan and Isaac that she is back so they can stop searching."

"My name is Henry. And please don't tell Isaac about Lucy returning. We must take her with us. Isaac has declared an attack on the Overworld. Your school is the only place that isn't aware of this because he has you isolated here."

Jane couldn't believe what she was hearing. She looked over at Lucy. "I'm sorry. You were right."

Phoebe asked, "Is there anything we can do to help?"

Henry replied, "We need you to spread the message that Isaac is behind these attacks here at the school. And Lucy has to come with us. We have a battle in the Overworld and we need her help. She will be a target if she stays here. They know she has left the campus and she knows about Isaac and his attack."

Jane said, "But nobody will believe us. Look at how we reacted when Lucy told us, and we are her friends. How can we convince a school full of strangers that our headmaster is a griefer?"

"It's not going to be easy, but you have to do it," Lucy told her.

Max looked at Phoebe and Jane. "It's not pretty in the Overworld. Isaac has staged daily zombie invasions and he has summoned the Ender Dragon in many villages."

Henry added, "At night, he has men in blue suits place TNT all over the towns, and they blow up various buildings. The attacks are very random and we have no idea who is going to be targeted. This puts us all on edge. It's awful."

Before Phoebe and Jane could respond, Lucy TPed with Henry, Max, and Adam.

Chapter 13
ZOMBIE INVASION

"You're back!" Steve was happy to see his friends. The town was in the middle of a serious zombie invasion and he needed their help. Zombies were ripping doors from their hinges and the townspeople were too exhausted to fight. The daily battles had intensified and left them depleted. Many of the villagers were transformed into zombie villagers. Steve tried to help the zombie villagers transform back into regular villagers with the help of golden apples, but he needed help.

Henry battled two zombies. Lucy was in the middle of her own battle with three zombies.

Kaboom!

There was an explosion in the distance. "What's that?" shouted Lucy.

"We don't know," Steve said as he slammed a zombie with his diamond sword. "It happens every night. We never know what the damage is until the morning. Many homes and businesses have been destroyed. And we don't have time to rebuild them because we are too busy battling this neverending zombie invasion."

"That's awful. We will put a stop to this," Lucy said as she continued to battle zombies. Adam splashed potions and tried to help his friends as the sun came up.

"The sun is up," Adam remarked. "We're saved!"

"The sun coming up is meaningless. There are constant rain showers during the day and more zombies spawn. It's not just a nightly attack. We have continuous attacks throughout the day," Steve told them.

Lucy said, "That was happening at school, too. We were attacked all day."

"Isaac has to be stopped," Steve announced.

"Why did I leave school? He's there. If we go back, we can stop him," said Lucy.

"That's true. We should go back to the school," Adam agreed.

"But first you need to help us. We have to find the zombie spawner," Steve said. "You found it before. Also, you must help us build an iron golem."

Lucy said, "Okay, we will help you find the spawner and build the golem. But once that is done, you have to help us and return to the school. We need to stage an attack on Isaac at the school. Hopefully, Phoebe and Jane have convinced the other students that Isaac is bad."

"That's not going to be easy. Look at how hard it was for you," Adam said to Lucy.

"What does that mean?" asked Steve.

Lucy explained how she had overheard Isaac talking to the men in blue suits in the Nether about an attack on the Overworld, but nobody believed her.

"Wow, that must have been hard," Steve said.

"Yes, it was really hard when Adam didn't even believe me." Lucy looked over at Adam.

"I said I was sorry." Adam didn't want to go over this again.

"I know," said Lucy. "Let's start building the golem."

They headed into town and picked a spot to build the golem. The gang pulled the supplies they needed from their inventories and started on the golem. It didn't take long until they were almost done. As they put the finishing touches on the golem, the sky turned dark and it began to rain.

"Oh no!" Lucy cried. "There are more zombies walking down the hill toward the town."

"I told you," Steve said as he took out his diamond sword. "This is relentless. We have attacks every day, and almost all day."

"Let's finish the golem," suggested Adam. "It's easier than fighting."

The group finished the golem, and the zombies didn't enter the village. Instead, they changed direction and walked toward houses off in the distance.

Kaboom!

"Not another explosion!" Steve was upset. "We still don't even know what was destroyed last night."

Their old friend, Kyra, sprinted toward them. "I need help. Someone blew up my house last night and now I have no place to shelter myself from the zombie invasion."

"Now we know what exploded last night," Steve said, and then told Kyra, "You can stay with me, but you have to help us fight."

The gang raced toward the zombies that were ripping doors off homes. They sprinted through the town holding their diamond swords. They were ready to end this battle of the zombies.

Kyra looked over Lucy. "I'm glad to see you again."

Lucy agreed and said, "I wish we were reunited under different circumstances."

The gang began to destroy the zombies, but the rain stopped. Steve said, "Do you see how we can never get anything done? The minute we start to battle the zombies, the battle ends. Then we begin to craft a golem or rebuild and we are attacked by zombies."

"I am going to find the spawner and then I'm going back to school. That is where we can stop this battle," Lucy told Steve.

"Okay. We finished the golem. Now we'll find the spawner," said Steve.

Chapter 14
THE OVERWORLD FIGHTS BACK

Finding the spawner wasn't as hard as they had imagined. "I found it!" shouted Lucy.

The spawner was in a cave. They used torches and broke the spawner to deactivate it.

"I need go back to school," said Lucy. She was shocked when Henry, Steve, Kyra, and Max told her that they'd be joining her.

Steve added, "We will help you battle Isaac. We will make sure the Overworld is protected."

"We don't have time to travel all the way to school," Adam informed them. "We need to teleport."

The gang teleported back to the school and into Lucy's dorm room. They were shocked when they saw Isaac standing in the room.

"I knew you'd return," Isaac told them.

Men in blue suits surrounded the gang. The men were carrying swords and were pointing them at the group. Lucy's heart was racing. She was incredibly nervous.

She took a deep breath and then splashed a potion of invisibility on the group. "Let's go," she said as she sprinted through the halls. The group followed closely behind; they they didn't want to lose her. Then Lucy spotted Phoebe and Jane. Men in blue suits surrounded them. She could hear them question her friends: "You know where Lucy is hidin!? You must tell us or we'll put you on Hardcore mode and destroy you. You don't want that to happen, do you?"

Phoebe looked terrified when she replied, "No, please don't put us on Hardcore mode."

Jane shouted at them, "Do whatever you want. We have no information. Lucy was in our room for a minute and then she disappeared. And we know how awful Isaac is and you can't shelter us from his dark plans anymore."

Lucy wanted to tell her friends that she was there, but she was invisible. She was happy to see that they were defending her and they believed her. But she didn't have time to stop and thank them, because she was sprinting toward Isaac's room with the others.

Lucy opened Isaac's door, but it was empty. She began to reappear. The potion had lost its potency. The others also began to reappear. Lucy could hear someone call for help.

"Help me! I'm trapped!" the voice called out.

"Where are you?" asked Adam.

"Who are you?" asked Lucy.

"It's Stefan. Isaac trapped me. He built a bedrock wall and trapped me behind it." Stefan's voice shook when he spoke.

Lucy spotted the bedrock wall by Isaac's bed. "How are we going to destroy a bedrock wall?" she asked her friends. Lucy knew that bedrock was extremely powerful.

"Should we use TNT?" asked Steve.

"No! That will destroy me!" Stefan sounded scared.

Lucy replied, "It doesn't matter if you're destroyed. You will just respawn in your bed. We can make sure we have someone waiting for you in your room. They will protect you from Isaac and his army of men in blue suits."

"Okay. Use the TNT," Stefan said weakly.

"We might need the cube of destruction. TNT might not work," Henry told them. He had experience trying to break through walls.

Lucy took out a couple of bricks of TNT she had in her inventory and ignited them, but they didn't break down the bedrock wall.

"We're going to use the cube of destruction," Henry told them. "Before we use it, I want Steve, Max, and Kyra to wait for Stefan in his room."

Steve, Max, and Kyra sprinted toward Stefan's room. They were going to help rescue him when he respawned.

"Stand back!" Henry warned them.

He unleashed the cube of destruction.

Kaboom!

Chapter 15
THE CREEPER ATTACK

Lucy, Adam, and Henry sprinted away from the blast and toward Stefan's room, but they stopped when they heard Max shout, "Watch out guys! Someone is spawning creepers!"

The halls were filled with the sneaky walking time bombs. One by one, the creepers started to explode. The creepers destroyed several students who were sprinting down the hall. Lucy knew that they would respawn in their beds, but it was still hard to see them destroyed.

Henry called out to Steve, "Do you have Stefan? Is he okay?"

They could barely hear Steve's reply. The sound of the creeper explosions was deafening.

"How are we going to get to Steve?" Lucy was dumbfounded. She wanted to sprint to her friends, but she knew it wasn't a smart move. If they sprinted down the hall, they would be destroyed by one of the exploding green creepers. She took out a potion. "We need to become invisible." She splashed the potion on her friends and they sprinted toward Steve and Max, making their way into Stefan's room.

Within seconds, they reappeared in front of their friends. Max and Steve were happy to see them.

Henry announced, "We need to find the creeper spawner."

Stefan said, "We need to find Isaac and stop him."

Max agreed, but added, "We need to get rid of these mobs. We aren't going to be able to defeat Isaac if we have to battle a series of hostile mobs. I don't want to get destroyed and respawn on the wheat farm. I am tired of TPing all over the Overworld. I want life to go back to normal. I want to go on a treasure hunt."

Henry said, "Max, we all feel the same way. And soon we will defeat Isaac and the battle will be over."

"I am in awe of your confidence." Stefan looked at Henry. "I hope what you wish for comes true."

"We all do," Kyra said. "And we are going to do something about it. Let's go find that spawner."

Lucy announced, "I only have a little bit of this potion left. This is our last chance to be invisible, so we had better make it work." She splashed a potion on the group, and they went to hunt for the spawner.

When they made their way past the creeper-filled hall, Lucy told her friends, "I bet it's in the basement, along with the zombie spawner."

Adam reminded Lucy, "Yes, remember when we were about to search down there? I bet there is a spawner in the basement."

The group sprinted as fast as they could. They wanted to reach the basement before the potion of invisibility wore off. As they sprinted, Lucy noticed Phoebe and Jane battling a group of vicious zombies. She wanted to call out to them. She wanted to help them battle the zombies. She wanted them to know that she was on the job and was trying to deactivate the zombie spawner, but she couldn't say anything. She had to sprint toward the basement.

"Down here," Max shouted as he began to reappear.

The gang followed him. Kyra called out, "What do you see?"

"I see—" Max began, but Henry interrupted him.

"Watch out!"

A horde of creepers emerged from a room. Max narrowly avoided being destroyed. Henry splashed potions on the creepers.

Kaboom!

The creepers exploded.

Max shouted, "I see the spawner. We need torches. Steve, help!"

Steve was the type of person who always had a full inventory. He grabbed torches and handed them to Max.

Max used torches to deactivate the spawner.

"Great job," Steve said, and the other agreed. But they were shocked when they heard a voice call out in the distance.

"Yes, you did a great job deactivating a spawner. But that is a very small accomplishment. I have staged a battle in the Overworld. In fact, as we speak, many towns are being completely destroyed. You will need a much bigger army to defeat me." Isaac laughed a sinister laugh.

"You aren't going to get away with this." Lucy shouted at the headmaster. "And I have no idea why you want to destroy the Overworld. When I was accepted into this academy, I was so proud of myself and so eager to learn. Now I am just disillusioned and upset. I trusted you. I thought you were going to teach me things and help me become more skilled at developing my talents in the Minecraft Universe, but now I see you are nothing but a sad, mean person. You have let your skills fill you with false power. You aren't nice."

Isaac just laughed at Lucy and sprinted toward her with his diamond sword, "You think you know how to play the game? Well, you don't. I know what the Overworld is really like. And I am going to be the head of the Overworld."

Stefan took out his bow and arrow and aimed at Isaac. "I know if I hit you, you'll just respawn in your room and escape, so I am not going to bother wasting an arrow on you, but I will tell you that I agree with Lucy. You are a disappointment."

"I'm glad you guys all agree about how bad I am. But I don't really care. And I am going to win this battle." Isaac let out another laugh, but stopped when he heard voices in the distance.

Chapter 16
TEACH, DON'T TERRORIZE

"You aren't going to get away with this," a voice called out.

Lucy looked over and spotted Phoebe standing in front of a large army of students. They were all dressed in armor and had diamond swords in their hands.

Phoebe said, "Your big mistake was picking the most skilled players in the Overworld to attend Minecrafters Academy. We have created an army of protectors of the Overworld. We are going to stop you and all griefers. That is the new mission for this school."

Phoebe advanced toward Isaac and pointed her diamond sword against his unarmored body. "You need to learn how to teach, not terrorize."

Isaac stared at them. "Um . . . I . . ." He could barely get any words out.

Jane stood next to Phoebe, "You don't seem so confident now. Where is that famous sinister laugh?"

Isaac put his head down. "I'm sorry. I just wanted more power."

"You had power. And you were using it to educate. Why did you become a bad guy?" Phoebe asked Isaac.

He had no response. He was also trapped. He had to surrender. Isaac only had one chance to get away.

Someone shouted, "The Ender Dragon has been summoned. It's flying around the campus. We must destroy it."

Students sprinted outside to help defeat this deadly dragon. Lucy and her friends were about to join them, but they noticed Isaac trying to escape in the chaos.

Lucy called out to Isaac, "Where do you think you're going?"

Phoebe and Jane raced toward Isaac with their diamond swords. Phoebe said, "We have enough people to destroy the Ender Dragon. You're not getting away."

Phoebe, Jane, and Lucy took Isaac outside to see the battle. The campus was filled with skilled fighters, who used snowballs, arrows, and strikes from their powerful diamond swords to destroy the flying menace. When the Ender Dragon was destroyed, a portal to the End spawned on campus.

"We aren't going to the End," Max announced. "We need to stay here and craft a prison for Isaac."

Lucy said, "We need students to travel around the Overworld to destroy the spawners in each town. We also have to let everyone know that the battle is over and Isaac has been caught."

Phoebe suggested that she build the prison. "I am very comfortable building structures."

Eitan walked over to Phoebe. "Yes, you are a skilled builder, but I've watched you flourish during your brief time at Minecrafters Academy. You are now a strong fighter and fearless warrior, too."

Phoebe was pleased. "Thank you. And I will be honored to build the prison."

Phoebe assembled a team and began to build the prison. Others were chosen to go out into the Overworld and spread the message that the battle was over and everyone could continue with their lives.

Phoebe and Jane walked over to Lucy. Jane said, "I want to apologize again for not believing you when you told us that Isaac was a griefer."

Lucy replied, "It's okay. There were times when I didn't believe it myself. I wanted to trust Isaac. I wanted to learn and focus on my studies and not get involved in any battles."

Phoebe said, "Well, you saved the school."

Lucy smiled.

Chapter 17
THE TRUTH

The teams were chosen to go out in the Overworld and deactivate the spawners. Max, Henry, Steve, and Kyra were going to save their town and all the villages they would visit on the way home.

Lucy was upset that her friends were leaving. It was so hard to say good-bye. "I'm going to miss you guys. It's so hard to say good-bye twice."

Henry smiled. "But now that this battle is over, you'll be able to finally study at Minecrafters Academy and will learn all the skills you wanted to learn. Next time you see us, you'll be a better player."

"I know, but it's still hard to say good-bye."

Kyra agreed and added, "But it had been so long since I had seen you. I'm happy that we had this chance to be reunited, even though it was under such awful circumstances."

Lucy smiled at Kyra. "Next time we meet, it will be a party."

"Good idea," exclaimed Steve. "We will throw a huge graduation party for you. And you can invite all of your new friends from school."

"That sounds like the best plan ever." Lucy was thrilled, but she was also sad to say good-bye.

"We can't make this a long good-bye. There are towns that are in desperate need of our help," Henry reminded them.

Lucy stayed behind at school and helped Phoebe and Jane construct Isaac's prison, while the others took off to finish saving the Overworld.

Adam led a team of students through the Overworld. Before he left, he told Lucy, "I'm excited to put my skills to use. But I'm also looking forward to coming back to school. I can't wait until they hire a new headmaster and we can start taking classes again."

Lucy agreed. "I'm glad the truth is out and now we can put Isaac in prison and move forward. I want to be able to have dinner with you in the dining hall without the fear of a blackout and a zombie invasion."

Adam agreed and set off on his journey through the Overworld.

Lucy walked over to Stefan, who stood next to Isaac and held a diamond sword against Isaac's chest.

Stefan was talking to Isaac. "You see what chaos you caused? But I'm glad these students were strong enough to fight you. You will now be an example at Minecrafters

Academy of how our students fight for good and not evil."

Isaac didn't try to defend himself. He stood next to Stefan and said nothing.

The prison was completed and Stefan led Isaac to his chamber. Isaac entered and climbed into bed. He pulled the covers over him.

As Stefan locked the prison door, he asked Lucy, "Will you help us find a new headmaster?"

"Don't you want the job?" asked Lucy.

"No, I'm not cut out for running an entire school. I'd rather work with the students," Stefan confessed.

"Then I will help you find a trustworthy headmaster." Lucy smiled.

"Thanks. I know you'll do a good job."

Lucy asked, "Can my friends Phoebe and Jane also help search for the new headmaster?"

"Of course." Stefan smiled.

Phoebe stood outside the prison she had constructed. Lucy walked over to her. "You did a good job with the building."

"Thanks." Phoebe was pleased.

"I'm glad we're friends again." Lucy looked at Phoebe.

"Me too." Phoebe smiled.

Chapter 18
BACK TO SCHOOL

The search for the new headmaster wasn't as easy as Lucy had imagined. She helped Stefan interview many candidates for the job. They finally settled on a woman who lived in the desert biome. She was an expert on all desert skills. Lucy was impressed since she was always having trouble trying to unearth treasures in the various desert temples that she encountered on her treasure hunts.

Stefan said, "Thanks for helping us pick a new headmaster. Classes will resume very soon. We have to wait for the other students to return and for the new headmaster to arrive."

Lucy was relieved the battle was behind them. "I can't wait to start classes." She noticed Eitan walking across the campus. She was excited for Eitan to teach her how to navigate her way around the Nether.

Until the new headmaster arrived, Lucy and her friends were able to relax. They were also very excited to see many of the students return to Minecrafters Academy. Every student had a different tale about deactivating the spawners. Students traveled throughout the Overworld and told stories about meeting new people in the towns. Lucy was especially happy when she saw Adam return to school.

Phoebe, Jane, and Lucy were in their dorm room when Adam came by and announced that he was back.

"Is the Overworld back to normal?" Lucy asked.

"Yes, thanks to you," replied Adam.

"I didn't do it alone. The Overworld wouldn't be safe and Isaac wouldn't be punished if I didn't have such amazing, trustworthy friends."

Phoebe and Jane smiled.

Lucy looked at all of her friends and smiled. "I'm excited to start classes and go back to school."

Everyone agreed. They were ready to go back to school.

DO YOU LIKE FICTION FOR MINECRAFTERS?

Check out other unofficial Minecrafter adventures from Sky Pony Press!

Invasion of the Overworld

MARK CHEVERTON

Battle for the Nether

MARK CHEVERTON

Confronting the Dragon

MARK CHEVERTON

Trouble in Zombie-town

MARK CHEVERTON

Available wherever books are sold!

AVAILABLE NOW FROM WINTER MORGAN AND SKY PONY PRESS

Treasure Hunters
in Trouble

The Skeletons
Strike Back

Clash of the
Creepers

Available wherever books are sold!